REAL LIVES

Noor Inayat
Khan

D0569527

For Simon

First published 2013 by
A & C Black, an imprint of Bloomsbury Publishing Plc
50 Bedford Square, London, WC1B 3DP

www.bloomsbury.com

ISBN 978-1-4729-0013-5

A CIP catalogue for this book is available from the British Library.

Printed and Bound by CPI Group (UK) Ltd, Croydon CR0 4YY

3 5 7 9 10 8 6 4 2

REAL LIVES

Noor Inayat
Khan

Gaby Halberstam

A & C BLACK
AN IMPRINT OF BLOOMSBURY
LONDON NEW DELHI NEW YORK SYDNEY

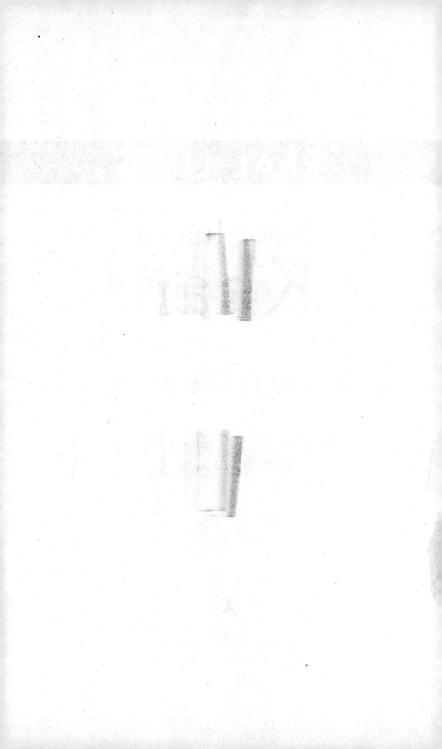

Prologue

13 September 1944

The icy fingers of dawn touched the bars of the prison cell, before feeling their way to the body of the young woman slumped across the cement floor. In the grey light, the blood in which she lay shone dully. From outside there came the sounds of shouting, the smart rhythm of hard heels on hard surfaces, and moaning. But inside the cell, the woman said nothing. The Nazi officer standing over her dealt her another kick, half-hearted this time. As though she were no longer worth the effort. Wiping his brow on his sleeve, he took his pistol from its holster.

'Kneel!' he ordered in his coarse French accent, shoving her feet with his boot.

1

16 June 1943

The pilot shut the plane, climbed into the cockpit, and they were off. Noor Inayat Khan waved to Miss Atkins through the window. She'd been overseeing Noor almost like a head mistress, and it was she who'd brought Noor to Sussex to catch the plane to France, and the beginning of her adventure.

The English Channel glittered in the moonlight like a sequinned scarf. In the time it took to fly from England to the airfield near Paris, Noor had to take on her new identity. She reached for the documents inside her bag. The photograph on her new ID card was definitely of her: brown eyes, heart-shaped face and darkish skin, brown-black hair cut in the latest Parisian style. But the name on the card was Jeanne-Marie Renier, a children's nurse. She'd been given a new birthday, too. Noor smiled: when the plane had taken off, she'd been twenty-nine, but when it landed she'd be twenty-five. Jeanne Marie was her new official name, but her code name was Madeleine.

The other things in her bag were more frightening. Miss Atkins had given her a Webley pistol. It was cold to the touch. She'd have to use it if the plane were met by the enemy. The thought of that was enough to make Noor shudder.

Next to the pistol, in a little envelope, were the four special pills to be swallowed if she were in trouble. The first would keep Noor awake if she needed to keep going. If she were captured, she could swallow the second pill and it would make her seem ill. The third could be put into the enemy's drink to make him sleep for six hours. That would give Noor a chance to escape. The fourth pill was the one she could use if she was absolutely desperate: the L pill. It contained cyanide, which was deadly. If she bit through the rubber coating and swallowed the poison inside, she would die within minutes.

Quickly, Noor closed her bag, and looked out of the window again. This was the start of her mission – a secret mission. She was a member of SOE, the Special Operations Executive. Winston Churchill, the Prime Minister, had set it up. 'Set Europe ablaze', he'd said, and that was what she and the other SOE agents were going to do.

They were going to work with the Resistance, the men and women working in secret to disrupt and destroy the Germans.

Did Churchill know about her? she wondered. The thought made her sit up straight. Not even Amma, her mother, nor her sister and two brothers knew where she was and what she was doing.

'We're nearly there,' the pilot said, his crackly voice breaking into her thoughts. 'Another ten minutes or so.'

She fluttered her fingers across her lap. She used to play the harp when she was younger; now she was known as a pianist. But that didn't mean that she played the piano. No, she was a wireless telegraph operator, someone who typed out messages in code on a radio set – the first female operator to be flown into France.

She would receive messages from London about agents coming to France, or when and where guns and ammunition would be dropped. When London planned acts of sabotage, it would be her job to pass the details on to the Resistance, and to report back on whether the agents had been successful, or whether anyone had been captured by the Germans.

Through the window Noor could see the lights marking the landing strip for the plane. There was a rattling and banging as they landed. Moving quickly, the pilot opened the door, and Noor scrambled down the ladder he lowered.

'Madeleine?' someone on the ground asked.

Just as Miss Atkins had said, there were two men waiting. One of them pushed a bicycle towards her.

'Take the train to Paris,' he said. 'Station is that way.' He pointed. 'Keep following the road.'

The two men disappeared into the night.

She was on her own. In the middle of nowhere. In enemy territory.

Panic grabbed hold of her, squeezing her ribcage until she could hardly breathe. What on earth had she been thinking when she'd agreed to do this?

The low mist weaving round her legs, and the chill wind, snapped Noor out of her fear. Pulling her green oilcloth raincoat round her, she pushed the bike towards some bushes. There was something she had to do. She knelt, glanced around, then, scrabbling at the soil, she dug a hole and threw the pistol in. If the enemy found it on her in Paris, she'd be arrested immediately. Maybe even shot.

She wiped her hands on her coat. She had to move off quickly. Someone might have seen the plane land. Someone could tell the Germans.

Noor leapt on to the bike, and began to cycle like crazy. There were very few houses and no lights. Was the clank-clank-rattle she could hear the mudguard, or her heart? Faster and faster she went. There were more buildings now, a church, the town hall, a boarded-up butchery. And finally, the station.

The clerk in the office was about to close up when Noor abandoned the bike and ran, panting, to buy a ticket. He stared at her before handing it over and pulling the blind down.

She went over to a map and timetable stuck to a wall. They were torn and stained. The timetable was dated 1941 – two years out of date. When would the next train to Paris arrive? Was there even a train? Noor wished she'd asked the ticket clerk, but he'd already left and the office was locked.

The platform was empty apart from a man in a coat with his hat pulled low, and one of the agents who'd met her plane. Noor moved towards him to talk to him. But he frowned and turned his back. She was on her own. Digging her hands into her pockets, her breath pluming in the cold air, she paced up and down.

Just as she thought there would be no train at all that night, the railway line rattled. Minutes later, the train arrived in a billow of steam. Noor climbed on board, and pulled the door shut. Sinking on to a seat, she hugged her arms around herself with excitement.

She was off to Paris, the city she loved more than any other. She couldn't wait to get there.

2

17 June 1943

It was morning when Noor's train arrived in Paris. Miss Atkins had given her the address of her contact – someone called Garry. It was such a lovely day, Noor decided to walk to the apartment, to breathe Paris in after the years she'd been away.

There were still the majestic buildings, the wide avenues, and the tree-lined boulevards. But it felt different. The people walking about looked miserable and wary. They kept their heads down, not wanting to catch anyone's eye. Many of the shops and restaurants were boarded up. Everywhere there were German signs, and banners with thick Gothic writing, and the black swastika like an evil spider.

A buzz came from behind her, growing louder. As she turned, six motorbikes roared up the road, ridden by German soldiers. The sunshine flashed off their helmets. They were followed by a procession of gleaming black motorcars, each one full of Nazi officers.

Noor's heart began to thud against her ribs.

As the last car drew near, an officer inside stared at Noor. His eyes were icy blue and piercing beneath his cap. A cold smile twitched his lips.

I am Mademoiselle Renier, Noor said to herself. *Jeanne Marie Renier. A children's nurse.*

Sweat gathered under her collar.

The car passed. Noor undid the top button of her blouse and pulled it away from her neck. That was the first time she'd actually seen the enemy, and the first time that the danger of her mission felt real.

Shivering now despite the warmth of the morning, Noor walked quickly to her contact's address.

She found the apartment block easily, and climbed the stairs.

'*Oui?* Yes?' A young man answered her knock. He opened the door just a crack.

For some reason Noor thought she'd be meeting an old lady. She was so surprised to see a man that she forgot to give her password.

'Er...I think I am expected,' she said.

After hesitating a moment, the man let her in. It was only after some confusion that Noor realised that he was Garry, her contact.

Quickly, she rattled off her password. It was more of a pass sentence, it was so long: '*Je viens de la part de votre ami Antoine pour des nouvelles au sujet de la Société en Bâtiment.*' This meant: 'I have come on behalf of your friend Antoine for news on the building society.'

'*L'affaire est en cours.* The business is in hand,' he replied, laughing. 'So you *are* Madeleine. For a moment there, I wasn't sure.'

The SOE divided agents into groups, called circuits. Henri Garry was head of the Cinema circuit. His fiancée, Marguerite, who lived with him, was also involved. They were both so friendly, it wasn't long before Noor was sitting down to dinner with them.

'So you know Paris well?' Marguerite asked Noor.

'Oh yes,' Noor said. 'Before... before Abba, my father, died and we moved to London, we lived in Suresnes. You know, on the outskirts of the city? Father named the house Fazal Manzil, which means House of Blessing. My brothers and sister and I had a wonderful childhood there.'

She smiled, thinking of their games in the garden, of singing songs with Abba, of playing her harp.

'My father was a Sufi priest,' she continued. 'He didn't believe in violence. People came from all over the world to listen to him.'

'Madeleine.' Marguerite reached forward and touched her hand. 'You mustn't go back to that house. It's far too dangerous. You might be recognised, and someone might betray you to the Germans.'

Noor nodded. 'Thank you,' she said, moved by Marguerite's concern.

'You know Cinema is part of a bigger circuit, called Prosper?' Garry asked Noor. 'Prosper has been very successful so far. Recently, agents sabotaged the power station at Chaingy in the centre of France, and destroyed some of the power lines. Prosper also attacked German goods trains, and derailed them. Took out a number of Gestapo – don't have the numbers yet.'

Noor thought about what he was saying. She would be part of all this soon.

'And we're planning many more attacks,' Garry continued. 'You'll be working closely with the head of Prosper, and his radio operator, Archambaud. You can use his radio set until yours is parachuted in.'

He took a pot off the stove, grimaced as he poured some dark liquid out of it into a cup, and pushed the cup towards her.

'Not coffee, I'm afraid. It's a hideous mixture of roasted barley and chicory, but it's all we can get. I can't remember when I last had a proper cup of coffee.'

He was right. It tasted awful.

'But at least it's hot,' Noor said. 'And maybe if you don't expect coffee you won't be disappointed.'

'That's the spirit,' Garry said with a smile, sitting down again. 'So, in the next few days, I'll be introducing you to the agents. Probably, meet France Antelme first. He's head of Bricklayer circuit. And – '

'I think that's enough for one night.' Marguerite put her hand on Garry's arm. 'Poor Madeleine looks exhausted.'

She turned to Noor. 'Why don't you stay here tonight? We have a spare bedroom. It's very small, but the bed's comfortable.'

Noor really was worn out, and her head was spinning. She sank into the soft bed. So this was the beginning of her adventure. It was dangerous – radio operators didn't last long – and people would be depending on her. Was she up to the job?

3

June 1943

Over the next few days, the names Garry had mentioned to Noor became real people: in particular the tall Mauritian, France Antelme, and –

'Gilbert Norman! Or should I call you Archambaud? Is that really you?' She threw her arms around him. 'You haven't changed a bit since school. Heavens – how many years has it been?'

Norman laughed. 'Too many, Princess. You're looking lovely.'

Noor flushed. Not many people knew of her royal great-grandfather, Tipu Sultan.

'What have you being doing since school?' he asked.

'Oh, I studied music and then child psychology, and I've had some children's stories published.'

'And now you're a pianist like me?' Norman asked.

'Yes, I was called "Bang away Lulu" because of the way I bashed at the keys.' Noor smiled. 'But that's because I had chilblains and my fingers were sore.'

'I know you haven't received your radio yet, so you can use mine in the meantime.' Norman checked his watch. 'Let's go now. It's hidden in one of the greenhouses at Grignon, at the National College of Agriculture. When we're there I'll introduce you to some other members of Prosper.'

They travelled there by Metro. The college was rather grand and set in large grounds. Normally, Noor would have wanted to amble around, looking at the plants and enjoying the sunshine. But she needed to send a transmission to London.

Norman led her to a small greenhouse. There was a gardener digging up a flowerbed nearby.

'That's Maillard. He's one of us. Keeps watch while I transmit messages, picks up parachute drops. This is Madeleine,' he told the gardener, as they drew near.

'*Mademoiselle.*' Maillard tipped his straw hat before returning to his work.

Norman unlocked the greenhouse and opened the door. They stepped inside, and immediately the hot, damp air brought a film of sweat to Noor's skin. The radio set was kept in a suitcase hidden in some crates behind a stack of wooden boxes and fertiliser.

'I expect this is just like yours,' Norman said, hauling it out. 'Fourteen kilograms is heavy for me – but you're so petite, I don't know how you're going to manage to carry this around.'

Noor laughed. 'I'll be OK. I'm small, but I have hidden strength.'

Norman strung up the twenty-metre long aerial so she could transmit properly.

'It's all yours,' he said, standing back.

Noor was a little nervous transmitting with Norman looking over her shoulder. But she needn't have worried. Her message was short and accurate: she'd arrived safely. Miss Atkins would be relieved.

'We'd better get this packed up quickly and hidden again.' Norman knelt to put the radio set back in its case.

While he hid the set, Noor wandered over to one of the windows. She looked out without really seeing, as she wondered whether Miss Atkins would send word to Amma.

'Now, listen. German Intelligence is expert at tracing transmissions. It's less likely here because Grignon is kind of in the countryside.' Norman got to his feet and took her arm. 'But in the centre of Paris, watch out. They drive around in vans disguised as bakers or delivery men. Anyone could be Gestapo, wired up to detect signals. They could be on to you within twenty minutes of your starting a transmission.'

'Thank you, Gilbert,' Noor said, quietly.

He patted her hand, and locked the greenhouse behind them. 'Professor Balachowsky and his wife and some of the other agents are waiting to meet you. The Prof's a biologist, and a member of Prosper.'

Norman took her over to their rooms in the College. The Professor and his wife, and the other lecturers and agents were so friendly, Noor felt immediately at home. She sat and chatted, and went to help in the kitchen, before carrying the tray of tea things into the sitting room.

'So, milk for everyone,' she said, kneeling at the table as she poured the tea. 'Sugar, or should I say saccharin?'

There was silence. Norman and Madame Balachowsky exchanged glances.

'What's wrong?' Noor asked.

'You're preparing tea in the English way,' Madame Balachowsky said. 'In France, we put the milk in last.

That is the sort of thing that would betray you to the Germans. You need to be careful, my dear.'

Who would have thought such a small thing could be so important? Noor went quiet for a while, embarrassed at her mistake. She drank her tea, then helped clear up. She was in the kitchen telling Madame Balachowsky about Amma, when the Professor appeared in the doorway, looking serious. He beckoned her into the passage.

'I found this in the entrance hall.' He held out Noor's portfolio containing all her security codes. 'If the wrong person got hold of these, we could all lose our lives. So could many others who trust us.'

First the tea, now this. Why was she being so scatterbrained?

'I'm sorry. It won't happen again.' She took the portfolio.

'Suspect everyone of being a spy. Give nothing away about what you're doing. Trust no one.' The Professor's brow was deeply furrowed. 'The Gestapo are everywhere, and there are many people who would gladly pass on information about us for money.'

Noor nodded. The Prof patted her arm, and they returned to the lively group in the sitting room. It wasn't long before Noor relaxed again. The sun shone through the long windows, and the food was good. It was a peaceful, lazy Sunday afternoon.

Not one of them knew just how close the Nazi menace was.

4

June 1943

That evening, a message came through from London: Noor's radio set, her suitcase and a new agent were to be parachuted into France. She couldn't wait to have her own clothes instead of borrowing Marguerite's. But more than that, Noor was excited about receiving her own radio set.

When Noor turned up at Grignon a couple of days later, Maillard, the gardener, was waiting for her outside the greenhouse. She waved and trotted over to him, delighted to see her battered leather suitcase at his feet. It was full of clothes that had been made especially for her in London in Parisian styles, down to the way in which the buttons had been sewn on.

'Thank you!' she said, taking it from him. 'I've been waiting for this. So the parachute drop went well?'

Maillard frowned. 'No. Your suitcase hit a tree. Everything spilled out. Archambaud had to pick it all up.'

Noor threw her head back and laughed at the thought of her dresses and underwear festooning the branches and scattered over the field, and Norman scampering about collecting them together.

Maillard wasn't so amused. 'You've got your suitcase,' he said. 'But the agent we were expecting has disappeared. The only sign of him was his parachute folded up and left on the ground. This is not good.' He drummed his hoe into the soil several times. 'Worse than that – four agents were supposed to turn up at Gare d'Austerlitz. No one appeared.'

Agents failing to turn up could only be bad news. Noor's stomach clenched.

'And my radio equipment?' she asked.

'It's been taken to Le Mans. You'll receive it soon.' He turned back to his flower bed. '*Faites attention*, be careful,' he said, his voice thick and gruff.

'I'll be back later this week. With Archambaud.' She took her suitcase. The joy of having her own clothes had evaporated.

Two days later, she went to Norman's apartment. She buzzed to be let in, glancing around in case she was being watched. The street was empty apart from a few scraggy pigeons scratching in the gutter.

No one answered.

'Not like Norman to forget,' she muttered. She set off for Grignon once again, hoping he might be there.

It was dusk when she arrived. She made her way to the greenhouse, only to find it locked, with no sign of Maillard either. She walked over to the Professor's office. It was open, but no one was in. The sitting room was tidy, and the kitchen was clean, the tea towels folded over the oven door handle.

Noor stepped outside again. What should she do? It was getting late. The Nazis had imposed a curfew on the people of Paris: no one was to be on the streets after midnight. Most people hurried home much earlier, not wanting to be out after dark. Encountering German soldiers in daylight was bad enough. There was a room at the College that the Professor had said she could use, so Noor hurried there to stay the night.

She slept badly. Norman kept popping up in her dream, telling her he wanted a quiet life. Maillard appeared, too, in a hat that looked as though it had been pulled out of the earth. *Faites attention, faites attention, faites attention*, he said in his gravelly voice.

She woke early the next morning and hurried over to the greenhouse. The sun was shining. Butterflies fluttered amongst the roses, and the air smelled of damp soil. It felt normal. Perhaps everyone had just been busy the day before. Perhaps Norman would be there, transmitting, blissfully unaware of having missed their appointment.

Once again, the greenhouse was locked. Noor pressed her nose against the glass, but the place was empty. Where on earth was Norman? She sat on a bench to wait.

When there was still no sign of him after half an hour, Noor gathered her jacket and handbag, and stood up to leave.

'Madeleine – wait!' She turned to see who was shouting out her code name.

It was the Professor, running towards her, his hair wild and his face red. By the time he reached her, he was gasping for breath.

'Thank goodness you are here – ' he wheezed, bending over and resting his hands on his knees. 'Terrible news!'

5

26 June 1943

'What is it, what's wrong?' Noor asked, her heart thudding against her ribs.

The Professor could hardly get the words out. 'My wife – received a telephone call – the head of Prosper and seventeen other agents – arrested – '

'No!' she gasped, sagging on to the bench. 'And – and what about Norman?' She could hardly bear to ask.

The Prof shook his head.

'No, not Norman. But – we don't know – where he is.'

'When did this happen?'

'Two nights ago.'

Agents were told not to say anything during the first forty-eight hours after they were captured. That would give the others in their circuit time to hide themselves and anything incriminating. After that, if the torture became impossible to bear, they could say what they liked.

Noor leapt to her feet. The first forty-eight hours had almost passed. 'We must hide Norman's set. Right now! And his codes. He keeps them with it.'

His hands trembling, the Professor unlocked the greenhouse. Noor ran inside, the Prof following. Noor dragged the suitcase containing the radio set out from its hiding place.

'We'll bury it,' she said, running out towards the vegetable garden behind the greenhouse. 'Here!' She pointed to a bed of lettuces.

Noor grabbed a couple of Maillard's spades from a wheelbarrow, and together she and the Prof dug up the bed. They buried the suitcase and put the lettuces back. Noor disturbed the earth on the rest of the bed to make it look less conspicuous.

The Prof took Noor's arm, his hand still shaking, his eyes clouded with worry. 'You must leave. Now. Tell Garry what has happened. Warn the others. Be on your guard all the time.'

Noor left Grignon straight away. Where was Norman? Had the Germans got him too? A chasm was opening up in her stomach.

'*Mon Dieu!*' Garry exclaimed when he opened the door to Noor's frantic banging. 'What is the problem?'

As soon as he heard the news, he grabbed his keys and left with Noor to find Antelme. He'd gone away for the day so they waited for him outside his apartment, sitting with their backs against his door as the light drained outside.

Noor kept churning the news in her mind. How could it have happened? Eighteen arrested at once. Norman had said that the circuit had become too large. Why hadn't they listened? And the head of Prosper hadn't been happy that so many members of the circuit were in one place at the same time on Sunday. Someone must have been careless. Remembering her own thoughtlessness with her security codes brought a blush to her cheeks.

There was another possibility. Perhaps they had been double-crossed. The thought turned Noor cold.

Garry, too, was disturbed. His mouth was set in a tight line, and he hardly spoke. Every so often, he stood up and paced in front of the window.

Footsteps sounded on the stairs. Noor stiffened. Garry's hands fisted.

It was Antelme, the familiar purple beret on his head. His smile faded as he saw the anxiety on their faces.

He unlocked his apartment, ushering them into the tiny dining- and sitting room. Garry told him what had happened. The pallor caused by shock, together with the stark light cast by the bulb hanging from the ceiling, made Antelme look ghostly.

'Right,' he said, drumming his long fingers on the table as he thought. 'We need to move. But first I need to speak to a few people.' He picked up the telephone and put a couple of calls through. His voice was low and urgent. After hanging up, he pressed the heels of his hands into his eyes.

'OK. Garry, you will go into hiding. Madeleine, you will move to a new safe house. My friend Raymond has a studio flat for you. I'll move to the same address, stay with another friend – Germaine – in her apartment. '

Garry set off straight away. Noor waited with Antelme while he grabbed some clothes and documents and threw them into a bag.

Antelme's legs covered a lot of ground very quickly, and Noor had to trot to keep up with him. They needed to get off the streets before the curfew.

'Did you find out about my radio set?' she asked, as they made their way through the dark streets.

Antelme sighed. 'That's the only positive thing at the moment – your equipment is safe. It's being kept at Le Mans. You'll get it soon, but for the moment you need to lie low.'

'But there must be something I can do in the meantime,' she said.

They'd reached the apartment block where they'd both be staying. Antelme buzzed to be let in. He looked down at Noor, a tired smile flickering across his face.

'Yes, there is. I need to know what went wrong. Find out anything you can.'

'I'll go over to Grignon tomorrow,' Noor said.

6

27 June 1943

It was late afternoon the next day, and Noor was in the new apartment. The flat was just one small room, with a bed, a narrow wardrobe, and a tiny foldaway table and chair pushed against the wall. The recess in one wall was home to a miniature stove with two rings, and there was a loo and shower in a windowless space closed off from the rest of the room.

Two taps and a knock. Checking the spyhole, Noor opened the door.

'Any news?' Antelme said, stepping inside. He was pale, and his hair was ruffled.

'I went to Grignon, saw the Prof,' she said. 'He didn't know who put the call through. He looked terrible – ashen and wild-eyed. He told me not to come back there ever again.' She gave a weak smile. 'It upset me. But, I understand. It would just be too dangerous for all of us. What've you found out?'

Antelme pulled out the chair and sat down. He took up most of the space in the room.

'I spoke to another member of Prosper circuit. It seems the Gestapo, after arresting Norman's girlfriend, marched into her apartment and seized her radio set.'

Noor gasped. 'And – and Norman? Any news of him?'

'Apparently, something bad happened in his apartment. His friends' things were all over the place, there was a meal left unfinished on the table, and no sign of them. Seems they left in a hurry. Norman's bed hadn't been slept in, and the bike he'd just borrowed was still there – but some of his stuff had been removed.' Antelme wiped his hands down his face. 'I'm pretty sure the Gestapo got him.'

'Oh, no.' Noor sagged on to the bed.

Antelme stood up. 'We have to press on, Madeleine. You'll soon have your radio set. But you must lie low. We don't know what the Germans have been able to find out.'

He meant that the captured agents would have been tortured. Some of them might have cracked. Might have revealed Noor and Antelme's identities to the Nazis. Panic clawed at her heart.

'I'm off,' he said. 'I'll be upstairs at Germaine's if you need me.'

Noor closed the door behind him. She locked and bolted it, even though there was little point: the Gestapo could break it down with one kick. Her hands still trembling with shock, she made herself a cup of coffee – or the bitter stuff that stood in for it – and poured in a load of sweetener.

It was dusk. Time to black out the windows. She drew the curtains, switched on a lamp, and sat at the table, wrapping her hands around the hot cup.

If the Germans caught her, what would she do?

Noor closed her eyes for a moment, carrying herself back to the beautiful gardens at Fazal Manzil, to Abba's soft voice, and the lessons he'd taught her and her siblings.

If the Germans caught her, the first thing they'd want would be her security checks. Then they could transmit to London pretending they were her. They could fool the British, spoil their plans, and capture more agents.

If Abba were alive, what would he say she should do?

It was as clear to her as if Abba were standing in front of her, calling her by the name she'd been given by her nurse when she was a tiny baby: 'Babuli, the worst sin of all is lying.'

It would be lying to give the Gestapo false security codes or false names.

So what should she do: betray her fellow agents? Or lie?

Betray. Lie. Betray. Lie.

Noor stood up and began to pace the gloomy room again. The words became a mantra, falling into the rhythm of her strides.

Stop! she ordered herself.

She halted in front of the mirror above the table, drawing herself up to her full height of one metre and sixty centimetres. The eyes staring back at her were bright and fierce.

Not for nothing was she the great-granddaughter of Tipu Sultan, the ruler of the Kingdom of Mysore in southern India. He was known as the Tiger of Mysore, a proud and brave commander; his blood ran through her veins.

She would rather die than lie. At the same time, she would not betray her fellow agents.

The Germans were close, and getting closer. If she were caught she knew exactly what she would do.

7

July 1943

Noor's room had begun to feel like a cell. She'd been out only to attend the small wedding of Henri Garry and Marguerite, and to buy food. She still hadn't received her own radio set, and she was desperate to bring London up to date.

She leapt to her feet. Decision made. She was going to Grignon to transmit – despite what the Prof had said about not coming back. She'd dig up Norman's set on her own if necessary. After all, she had a job to do.

Noor moved quickly, happy to get out in the warm sunshine. Germaine had lent her a bicycle, which she collected from the rack at the back of the building.

Wheeling it along the pavement, Noor stopped outside a grocery shop. There was a shortage of fresh fruit and vegetables in Paris; a queue of mainly women and old men straggled out of the shop and on to the pavement. Noor pretended to inspect the boxes of wizened turnips. Antelme had told her not to draw attention to herself, to look as normal as possible to anyone who might be watching her, and she hoped she looked like any housewife going about her business.

After a moment or two, she walked on, the bicycle wheels ticking like a speeding-up clock. A troupe of German soldiers approached, their grey-green uniforms ugly against the buildings she loved so much. Despite her thudding heart, Noor forced herself to slow down.

'*Schönes mädchen!*' one of them called out to her. '*Belle!*'

He was telling her she was beautiful. Noor smiled and tossed her head, trying to play the part of a carefree Parisienne, all the while hoping her shaking hands wouldn't betray her, and willing the soldiers to move on.

The soldier waved and leaned in towards his friends, their heads together as they whispered and laughed.

Noor kept smiling until they'd passed. Still trying to look casual, she stopped at a bakery, and joined the queue to buy a couple of dusty rolls. She threw the bag into her basket, furtively checking that she wasn't being watched, or followed.

She turned the corner. The street was empty apart from a very old lady polishing a brass door handle. Noor leapt on to the bike, and cycled as fast as possible towards Grignon.

The gates to the College were wide open. Nothing unusual in that. But the gravel drive was deeply rutted: heavy vehicles had driven in. The grounds looked empty, with no sign of any of the gardeners. No sign of any students either. A wheelbarrow lay tipped over on its side, plants spilled out in a messy heap. Was that the brim of Maillard's straw hat sticking out beneath them?

Something wasn't right. Noor got off the bike and wheeled it on to the path in the shade of the shrubbery beside the drive.

She emerged near to the main College buildings.

It took her a few seconds to take in what she was seeing: a fleet of shiny black Nazi cars in front of the College.

A guttural German voice barked from inside the building. Two heavy-set men strode out of the front door, dragging Maillard between them.

Noor flung the bike to the ground, and darted back into the shadows, hardly breathing. She made for the gates. Trying desperately not to draw attention to herself by running, she left the College and headed out on to the pavement. A bus drew up and she leapt on board, wheezing with panic.

8

July 1943

Back in the centre of Paris, Noor scurried through the streets until she reached her apartment block. She ran up the stairs, and hammered on the door of Antelme's flat.

Germaine opened it, her face stretched with fright. When she saw that it was Noor, she grabbed her sleeve and pulled her inside.

'You look terrible. What's happened?' Germaine asked. She let go of Noor, and shouted for Antelme, who stepped out of one of the rooms.

'Noor – speak to me. Where've you been? What's wrong?'

Stumbling over her words, and breathing in gasps, Noor told them what she'd seen at Grignon. Antelme looked grave.

'Someone's squawked,' he said. 'We're in more danger than I thought.'

There was a sharp tap on the door. The three of them looked at each other in alarm. Antelme pulled

Noor into the kitchen, while Germaine went to the door. Noor heard muttered conversation and the front door being shut.

'You can come out,' Germaine called. 'It's Jean Worms, head of Juggler circuit.'

Noor and Antelme stepped into the entrance hall. They all shook hands. Noor could see that Worms was very agitated. He kept pulling at his earlobe and blinking.

'The wife of one of our agents telephoned me,' he said. 'Bad news. She went back to their old flat with another agent. The Gestapo were there. Arrested the agent. Madame escaped.'

'Did they get anything?' Antelme asked.

Worms nodded. 'Your food card. She tore off the front page. Ate it. But the next page had your old address on it.'

Noor saw Antelme's face drain of colour.

'I have to go,' Worms said. 'Phone me later. I may have more news then. 6.30pm.'

He gave Antelme a scrap of paper with a number on it, and left.

'I've only been here two weeks,' Noor said. 'And it's all falling apart.'

'It's a house of cards,' Antelme said. 'Touch one, and the whole lot flutters down.'

'Try not to be too pessimistic.' Germaine went into the kitchen to make them all a cup of tea.

Noor felt too churned up to drink hers. Nor could she eat the biscuit Germaine had balanced on the saucer. She kept thinking of Maillard, and about Norman. What had the Germans done to them?

She pushed the cup away. 'I want to phone Grignon. I need to find out what happened, and to tell London.'

Antelme looked doubtful. 'OK... but leave it until later.'

Time passed slowly that afternoon. Noor went back to her flat. She washed some of her stockings and blouses, hanging them on chairs near the window to dry. All the while, she thought of the people she knew in the circuit: were Norman and his girlfriend together, at least? Was it he who had told the Germans about Grignon? Had he mentioned her?

The shadows lengthened, and a cool breeze fluttered her drying clothes. Noor couldn't bear to be alone with her thoughts any longer. She made her way upstairs, back to Germaine's flat.

Antelme opened the door.

'More bad news?' Noor asked as soon as she saw his pale face. A smell of something burnt hovered around him.

'The Gestapo have been to our arms depot near Trie-Château. A number of agents were arrested and killed.'

He pulled his hands down his face, distorting his eyes for a moment. 'Also, I went round to my apartment to see the caretaker. The Gestapo had been there looking for me. They asked her about me.' He gave a dry laugh. 'They described me down to my purple beret, can you believe?'

'What happened? Did she give you away?' Noor asked.

He shook his head. 'No. But they said they'd be back. I slipped into the flat, and burnt all my papers.' He paced up and down. 'They're on to me, Madeleine. I need to leave Paris. But, first, I want to speak to Worms.'

He put a call through. Noor saw Antelme's face fall as he talked, before he replaced the receiver.

'Spoke to someone in Juggler circuit. Worms is "ill", he said.'

A wave of cold swept over Noor's body. 'Ill' meant arrested. She could hardly believe it. He'd been standing there, in that flat, only a few hours earlier.

'Call Grignon.' Antelme stood aside so that she could phone. 'No. Call the Balachowskys' apartment, just in case the Gestapo are still at Grignon.'

Madame Balachowsky answered the phone. She spoke rapidly. Sixty German policemen had been at Grignon that morning. After interrogating the Director of the College, they arrested him, Maillard and six students. They pretended to shoot groups of students to frighten them into giving information. Finally, they released the Director with a warning.

'My husband says that's not the last we will hear from them,' she said. 'Now I must go. Call tomorrow for more news.' She put the phone down.

Noor was shaking. The Germans were picking the SOE agents off and the networks were falling apart.

'Madeleine, you look like you're going to faint,' Antelme said. 'Quickly, sit down.'

Germaine put her arm around her and sat next to her on the sofa.

'OK. Things are getting too hot here in the city. We need to get out,' Antelme said. 'I've spoken to Robert Benoist, of Chestnut circuit. He lives in Auffargis, about twenty-five miles from here. Chestnut receives weapons parachuted in from England. Its agents hide them in dumps in the forest round his estate. We'll stay with Benoist. Madeleine, pack a few things: you'll come with me, at least for a while.'

'But what about my radio set? It's still in Le Mans.'

Time was passing, and she was neither receiving nor transmitting messages. So much was happening. She had to warn London before more agents, more ammunition, and more supplies were dropped into France, only to be picked up by the Germans.

'Ah, of course.' Antelme rubbed his chin. 'I'll make sure you get it soon. But in the meantime, perhaps Benoist will arrange for one you can borrow.' He glanced over at Noor, a tired smile on his pale face. 'Cow pats and wild mushrooms – a bit of fresh air will do you the world of good.'

'I love the smell of the country,' Noor said, trying to smile, too.

She made her way back to her flat, glad there was now a definite plan, at least for the next couple of days. Glad, too, to be leaving the cramped room.

She threw a few things into the cloth bag which she slung over her shoulder. Not that long ago, she might have worried about how she looked, but there were far more important things to think about now.

9

July 1943

Noor and Antelme reached the Gare d'Austerlitz. People moved from the station like cats slipping into the shadows. Many were holding packages tightly against their sides: precious vegetables smuggled in from the countryside, butter, and lumps of meat, too. Noor wondered whether she could bring some fresh food back for Germaine, who'd been so kind to her.

The train journey from Paris didn't take long. They'd hardly stepped off the platform when Benoist swept up in a low-slung sports car.

'*Salut!*' he called out.

Leaning across, he flung open the passenger door for the two of them. 'Lucky you're so petite,' he said to Noor.

There was only one row of seats, so Noor found herself squashed between Benoist and Antelme. She hardly had time to introduce herself before Benoist put his foot down. They sped off with a ripping and grinding of stones, and a whiff of burnt tyres.

Noor knew he was a famous racing car driver, but she hadn't expected to find herself tearing down the road and careering round bends as if she were on the famous circuit at Le Mans.

It was terrifying, and exhilarating.

When they pulled up in front of Benoist's grand house, Noor was breathless. She put her hands to her hair to bring it back down to earth.

'*Oh la la!*' she laughed. 'I think we flew, rather than drove.'

Antelme replaced his beret. Even in the moonlight, Noor could see that he looked a bit green. 'Yes, that was quite a ride,' he said. 'Not many people can say they've been driven by a World Champion racing car driver.'

Benoist ushered them into the house, along a passage lined with photographs of racing cars, and down a flight of wooden stairs into a large, old kitchen in the basement. The walls were hung with gleaming copper pots and there were stacks of white china on shelves. Something was bubbling in a pan on the stove. It smelled of tomatoes, and rosemary, and garlic. There were two men and two women gathered round the long, scrubbed wooden table in the centre, their heads together as they looked at a map. They drew apart when Noor, Antelme and Benoist walked in, and turned to look at them.

One of the women stood up and took both Noor's hands in hers. 'You must be Madeleine. Come, sit down. We've been expecting you. Would you like a glass of wine?'

Noor shook her head. 'No, thank you.' The smell of the food was intoxicating and her stomach rumbled. 'A glass of water would be lovely, though.'

The other woman pulled out a chair and patted the cushion. 'So you're the wireless telegrapher for Cinema circuit?'

'Yes – well, I would be, if I had a set. I'm still waiting to receive mine.'

Someone clattered down the stairs, bursting into the room. '*Salut! Salut!*' he said.

'Ah, here's Dowlen, our pianist,' Benoist said, pushing a glass of water towards Noor. 'Perhaps Madeleine here can borrow your set?'

'Yes, of course,' Dowlen said. 'What's been happening in Paris?' He turned to Antelme. 'I heard there's bad news.'

51

Everyone leaned towards Antelme.

'Well,' he said, 'Prosper circuit is not prospering at all. In fact, it's in a mess. Same with the circuits in Gisors, Falais, L'Eporcé...The Gestapo are closing in, my friends. Who knows how much longer we shall all be free.'

The maid came into the kitchen. She took the lid off the pot, stirred the contents and brought it to the table. The mood round the table was sombre as they ate the vegetable stew. It was delicious, and fresh, but Noor was no longer hungry.

10

July 1943

The next morning, Noor put a call through to the Balachowskys' home. The housekeeper answered.

'*Non, mademoiselle*,' she said, her voice muffled. 'The Professor's not here.' She began to sob.

'What's wrong? What's happened?'

The housekeeper blew her nose. It was a minute or two before she could speak.

As soon as Noor put the receiver down, she hurried outside to find Antelme. He was sitting at a table going through a pile of documents.

'The Professor's been arrested. The Gestapo,' Noor said, panting. 'Taken him.'

Antelme jumped to his feet. 'Do you think he'll talk?' he asked. 'Stupid question, I'm sorry. Who wouldn't?'

'He and I – together we buried Norman's radio in the garden. We were in such a panic, we buried his security codes, too. If the Germans get hold of them – ' Noor didn't need to spell out the danger.

'OK. This is the plan. Please send a message to London: tell them about the arrests and the collapse of the circuit. Ask them to organise a flight back to England for me as soon as possible. The Germans know about me, I need to get out. Use Dowlen's set.'

Dowlen brought his radio set round that evening. He and Noor left the light and warmth of the kitchen and made their way into the grounds. The sky was clear of clouds; a few stars pierced the indigo sky. Noor breathed in the sharp scent of pine sap and damp soil. It reminded her of their garden at Fazal Manzil, when the night perfumes would tiptoe in through her open bedroom window.

An owl hooted, and a sneaky breeze rattled through the leaves, making Noor jump. Dowlen set up the aerial, looping it in the branches of a tree, while Noor stretched her hands over the keys of the radio set.

What if her fingers were stiff, or she'd forgotten how to do it?

She needn't have worried. Before long, she was tapping out her transmission as though she'd been doing it all her life. She remembered with some pride that she'd been the fastest operator during her training days. She relayed the bad news of all the arrests, and asked London to organise a flight back for Anselme as soon as possible.

As soon as she'd finished, she helped Dowlen pack the set away.

'OK?' Dowlen asked. 'Shall we go back inside? I feel like a cup of something hot.'

Noor rubbed her arms. It was a bit chilly, but she wanted to stay outside a little longer, on her own. 'I'll be along in a minute. I like the fresh air,' she said with a smile. She needed to think things through.

Dowlen patted her hand, picked up the suitcase, and made his way back inside.

Noor stepped on to the path that circled the house. The moonlight gave it a strange blue-white glow.

One by one the circuits were breaking down. Had someone spoken of her to the Nazis? Probably. Shivering, she looked up at the sky.

Should she call it a day and take the plane back to England with Antelme, before they got her too?

As if carried on the breeze, she heard Abba's voice: 'Babuli, remember the words of the Hindu poem, the *Bhagavad Gita*.' She could almost see the way his beard moved as he spoke, and the gleam of the heavy chain he wore round his neck. 'It is better to act than not to act, and better always to act selflessly.'

The SOE had trusted her to do her job. Hitler had occupied her beloved France, and was threatening England, the country which had given her and her family shelter. She owed Britain a duty, one she took seriously.

Noor made her way back inside. Her earlier agitation had disappeared, and calm had taken its place. She'd made her decision.

Back in the kitchen, she slipped into the chair beside Antelme.

'You seem – ' he looked closely at her ' – serene.'

'Yes,' she said. 'I've made up my mind. I'm going to retrieve my own radio, and operate from Paris. It's where I can be most useful.'

Early the next morning, after breakfast, she said her goodbyes. One of the women wrapped some potatoes and tomatoes in newspaper, and popped them into Noor's bag.

'Come back soon,' she said, giving Noor a hug. 'And look after yourself.'

'Yes, be careful,' Antelme said. 'Chances are the Gestapo know about you. They'll be watching out for your transmissions.' He walked with her to Benoist's car. 'You sure about this? You don't have to go back to Paris. You can stay here. Help the girls. Safer for you.'

Noor threw her arms around him. 'It's so sweet of you to worry about me. But I'll be fine. Who knows, I may even be safer in Paris than here. It's easier to hide there.' She climbed into the car, and he shut the door. 'I'll let you know when your flight will be.'

Benoist put his foot down and the car roared down the drive. It wasn't long before they'd reached the station.

'Just telephone me when you want to come back,' Benoist called out as she made her way to the ticket office. He blew her a kiss and drove off, followed by a billowing of dust.

11

July 1943

The train drew into Paris. Noor stepped out of the carriage and on to the platform a different person from the one who'd left just a few days before. She strode off towards the Metro, and her apartment, reaching it quickly.

The earthy and green smells of the potatoes and tomatoes in her bag reminded Noor she'd wanted to give Germaine a present. She trotted up the stairs and tapped on her door.

'Madeleine!' Germaine exclaimed. 'Tell me, is everything OK in Auffargis?'

'Yes, all's well there. I brought you these.' Noor handed her the package of vegetables.

Germaine buried her face in them. 'Better than Chanel perfume,' she laughed. 'Thank you, thank you!'

Noor smiled. 'When I go back in a week or so, I'll bring you more. May I make a couple of telephone calls, please?'

Her first call was to Madame Balachowsky, who could hardly speak to Noor, she was so upset. The Nazis had been back to Grignon, and the first thing they did was dig up the lettuces. The Prof must have talked.

A shudder rippled down Noor's spine. How badly must he have been tortured to have revealed the whereabouts of the radio set?

'Bad news?' Germaine asked.

Noor nodded. The Nazis had Norman's set, and his codes. London could easily be tricked into believing he was transmitting. Lives were in danger. She had to act fast.

Her second call was to the agent holding her radio set. A few hours later it was delivered to her apartment. Noor ran her fingers over the leather case, glad to have it back. She had work to do.

How fantastic would it be if she could build a new circuit? She could actually make a difference to the war effort.

Glancing around the tiny room, her eyes settled on the clothes she'd left to dry. She strode across the room, scooped up the blouses and stockings and flung them into her suitcase, along with a few other bits and pieces she'd taken out. She needed to be ready to move on at a moment's notice.

Antelme had given her various tasks, and she set about doing them as soon as possible. In the Tuileries gardens, there was a bench in the shade of some plane trees. It felt far from the Germans' speeding cars and motorbikes and the fear that prowled the streets of Paris.

The day after she returned, Noor made her way to this oasis to meet Vaudevire and Viennot, Antelme's contacts. They met there every few days over the following weeks. Noor passed on money Antelme had given her, and gathered valuable information from them to be sent back to London.

Apart from a fleeting return to Auffargis to say goodbye to Antelme in the middle of July, Noor stayed in Paris.

London had warned her not to transmit for a while, especially not from her apartment. There was no doubt now that the Germans knew of her. Their detection equipment was on the alert, waiting for her signals, ready to pounce. It was frustrating, but Noor knew she should heed London's warnings – at least for the while.

A few weeks later, London flew one of the heads of the SOE into Paris. He arranged to meet Noor.

'Bodington.' The man had plastered-down hair and round, horn-rimmed spectacles. He stretched out his hand to Noor. 'Major Nicholas Bodington. Here to see what has become of Prosper circuit.' His handshake was surprisingly floppy. 'One of the last remaining radio operators, I hear?'

Before Noor could answer, he continued. 'Very good.' He smoothed his little moustache. 'I'd been here only one week when Jerry nabbed the pianist who came with me. Trap. Thought it smelled fishy. Lucky escape for me, but I've no operator now. So, I need your help.'

'Yes, of course,' Noor said, smiling to hear his English accent, wanting to laugh when he called the Germans 'Jerry'.

'Where're you staying? How long've you been there?'

When Noor told him, he frowned. 'Too long in one place. Need to keep moving, my dear. Keep Jerry guessing.'

Bodington found her a flat near the Bois de Boulogne, the huge park to the west of Paris. In five minutes, her suitcase was packed. She said goodbye to Germaine, and she was on her way, suitcase in one hand, radio set in the other.

The Bois de Boulogne: Noor remembered it as a green and peaceful place. She and her family had had a wonderful picnic by the lake there one day, the sun making the water sparkle, and the grass dapple with shadow. It was dusk when she arrived at the apartment, and she was tired. She hardly took in the details of her new home, just grateful for a soft bed to fall into.

She woke the next day to the sound of boots tripping up and down the stairs. She opened her door a crack. Closed it immediately.

German officers.

12

August 1943

Noor couldn't believe it. Bodington had moved her into a block of flats rented by the SS.

The SS was the hugely powerful force that carried out most of Hitler's orders. What if they discovered who she was?

After a few hours' sitting on the floor with her back to the front door, not daring to go out, Noor gave herself a talking to. 'Get up. Act normally. This is the eye of the storm,' she told herself. 'The safest place. They wouldn't dream of looking for you here.'

She picked herself up, and left the building. With a carefree smile that hid her fear, she greeted several officers on her way out. They were polite, and not in the least suspicious of her. Feeling bolder, she set off for the café Bodington had bought as a meeting point for agents.

She was met with even more bad news.

They'd all assumed Auffargis would be safe. They were wrong. The Gestapo had swooped. They'd arrested everyone apart from Robert Benoist, who'd made a miraculous escape. They'd even beaten up Benoist's mother. The thought made Noor want to retch. Dowlen, too, had been grabbed, tracked down by the direction-finding vans. Of course, the Germans had found and seized all the hidden arms. Chestnut circuit was well and truly smashed.

Now Noor ignored the order to lie low. She was the only radio operator in Paris, and she threw herself into sending and receiving transmissions. Antelme sent her instructions from London: meet this person or that; arrange flights; collect money and pass it on to someone else for the financing of troops and arms; find out and relay information about military equipment.

It was August, and hot. Sweaty and exhausted, Noor raced across Paris with her heavy suitcase from one location to another, never staying still for long. The detection vans were out there, and they were after her.

She dyed her hair red, then blonde. She changed her hairstyle: middle parting, side parting, swept back, tied in a scarf. She wore dark glasses. She kept moving, always moving.

Needing different safe places from which to transmit, Noor contacted people she'd known when she was growing up. Could she trust them? Were they collaborators, working in secret for the Nazis? She had no way of knowing.

Dr Jourdan had looked after Noor when she'd been ill as a small child. He was pleased to see her when she knocked on the door of his Paris flat. He ushered her inside, beaming all over his gentle face. '*Cherie!*' he called his wife. 'Come see who's here!'

'*Mon Dieu,*' Madame Jourdan exclaimed, bustling into the hallway and taking Noor's hands. 'You are so thin. Too thin,' she said, leaning back to get a better look at her. 'Where's your lovely *maman*? And your brothers and sister? Are you back living here?'

Noor smiled. She felt she could trust them, and told them what she was doing.

Dr Jourdan looked very grave when he realised how dangerous her work was. 'You can use our house in the country to transmit,' he said. 'But only if you promise to take extra care of yourself.'

Madame Jourdan nodded. 'And you remember that little rose tree you gave us as a gift? We called it the "Noor Inayat". You will see that it is now as beautiful as you are.'

Noor travelled to their country house. Her tree had grown tall and strong, and it covered the front of the house in big pink roses. Noor picked a few, burying her nose in them to breathe in their scent, before putting them in her pocket. She longed for those innocent days, before Abba had died, before the war.

She wiped away her tears and set about transmitting.

She was glad to be able to use the house, but it was far from the centre of Paris, and she soon worried that she'd used it too many times. One day, back at her flat, she needed to contact Antelme urgently. She glanced out of her window. There was a tall tree just outside. It was evening. No one was about.

Not allowing herself to think about it too much, Noor flung the radio aerial out of the window. She ran outside and picked up the end of the wire. She was trying to throw it over a branch when there was a scrape of an upstairs window opening.

A German officer leaned out. '*Mademoiselle*,' he called down.

Her skin turned to ice.

'Would you like some help?'

Her heart thundering as hard and as fast as radio keys, Noor smiled her most innocent smile. 'Oh, yes please,' she said. 'That would be wonderful.'

Moments later he was downstairs with her, a cigarette dangling off his lower lip as he flipped the end of the aerial over the branch.

'*Voilà!*' he said.

'Thank you, thank you,' she said out loud, but her mind was scrambling to find an explanation if he asked her what she was doing. *I know – I'll say I want to hear some Wagner on my wireless. Need the aerial to pick up the radio station*, she thought.

He plucked the cigarette from his lip, and looked at her quizzically.

'Hermann!' someone called from the window.

The officer pretended to tip his cap, and wandered back upstairs.

Sweat soaking the back of her dress, Noor leapt back inside. She made her transmission extra brief. She'd taken a huge risk.

But it didn't stop her taking more.

13

September 1943

She'd been warned never to go back to Suresnes, the area of her childhood home. People would recognise her, could betray her. But, desperate for new places to transmit, she made her way there. The streets were so familiar, it was as though no time had passed. Noor found herself within a hundred metres of Fazal Manzil, her old house, when something made her stop.

Instead, she made her way to the house of an old family friend.

'Noor!' Madame nearly dropped the vase she was holding when Noor asked her if she could use her house. Pulling Noor inside, she whispered urgently, 'There are Germans everywhere. We're surrounded.' She took her to the kitchen, and pointed. 'See. Fazal Manzil. Occupied by Nazis.'

Noor felt ill to think of her lovely home so infested, and relieved that she hadn't gone there first.

Another old friend who lived nearby was happier

about Noor using her house. Soon Noor was appearing there every afternoon with her suitcase, taking a chance every time that someone might recognise her and report her.

Paris sweltered in the heat. Noor flitted between the different houses and meeting places, collecting information and passing it on, criss-crossing the city, becoming thinner and increasingly exhausted.

Her messages to London were extremely important. She told them about the German torpedoes that were being stored in the sewers, asked for explosives to be sent to the Resistance, helped agents escape to England, and arranged for false documents.

London had asked her to work with a man called Gieules to set up a network in the north of France. Noor introduced him to several agents in Paris, and set up a meeting for him with a British officer.

When she made it back to her apartment at the end of every day, she collapsed into the armchair – exhausted, but exhilarated, too. She was doing what she'd come to Paris for, and it made her feel proud.

14

October 1943

A week passed, and the weather, at long last, began to turn. Noor was at Viennot's apartment.

'I'm worried,' Noor said. 'I arranged for Gieules to meet that British officer at the end of September and I haven't heard a word from him since. He usually contacts me every day.' She paced up and down his kitchen. 'Do you think he's been arrested?'

'Madeleine, will you sit down. You're wearing yourself out with all this anxiety.'

Viennot tapped his cigarette on the edge of the saucer and dug through some scraps of paper from his pocket. 'Here's his number. Why don't you just telephone him?'

Noor put the call through. It rang seven times, and she was about to ring off when Gieules picked it up.

'Oh, thank goodness,' Noor said. 'You're there.'

Gieules cleared his throat. 'Yes. Yes, I'm here.' He paused a moment. 'Listen, Madeleine, we need to – to meet. I have something to give to you.'

'OK. Tell me where and when.' Why did he sound so distracted?

'Er...say, 10 am tomorrow...yes, ten, at the Etoile... at the corner of Avenue MacMahon and Rue Tilsitt.'

'Of course. See you there.' Noor put down the phone, frowning. 'Something's wrong. He sounded distant.'

Viennot collected Noor the next morning. She was glad he was coming with her: two pairs of eyes were better than one. She had a nagging sense that something was amiss, and she could see that Viennot was worried too.

'Wait here,' he said when they reached the Arc de Triomphe, not far from the meeting place. Noor hung back, stepping into the doorway of a boarded-up shop. She watched Viennot make his way down the Avenue.

Within minutes, he came trotting back, breathing heavily, his face red.

'Stay!' he hissed as she moved towards him. 'It's a trap. Gieules is there. Six guards, too. Waiting for you.'

Noor's heart hammered against her ribs. Gieules had betrayed her. A tremor of anger rippled through her fear. How could he have done such a thing?

But then she thought back to their telephone conversation. Perhaps there'd been a German pistol at his head. What would she do if she found herself at the end of a gun barrel?

Noor leaned out to watch as Gieules was pushed into a car. The doors slammed and the long black car sped off through the traffic. Her hands were trembling as she put them to her face.

'I can't believe how close that was. They nearly got me,' she said to Viennot. 'I think the Germans must know what I look like.' She touched her hair. 'Look at this. I've already dyed my hair so many times, it's turned into straw, and I'm beginning to resemble a scarecrow. I need a better disguise. Different clothes.'

She shifted from one foot to the other as Viennot looked at her from the top of her head to her shoes.

He sighed. 'OK, *vite,* quick. We can do something. Come with me.'

The hairdressing salon was a gold and pink place tucked away in a side street. It was quiet inside: thick rugs and velvet cushions absorbed all sounds. Noor's hair was poked at by a snooty lady, who then set about massaging, dyeing, smoothing, cutting, shaping and drying Noor's hair. She felt like a pampered poodle, but the hairdresser did a wonderful job. When at last she was allowed to look in the mirror, Noor saw how her hair was now as shiny, brown and sleek as a conker.

'*Magnifique*,' Viennot said when she emerged from the salon. 'And now what your new brunette hair needs is some new outfits. Follow me.' He tossed his silk scarf over one shoulder.

In an expensive boutique nearby, Viennot chose a tailored, crisp blue dress with a white trim for her, as well as a sweater, and a chic matching hat. She stepped out of the changing room to show him.

'*Fantastique*,' he said. 'Keep these clothes on, and pass me your old ones.'

He took Noor's raincoat and dress and stuffed them in a bin, then stood back to look at her properly.

'*Oh la la*, you look even more beautiful.' Noor blushed. 'Still worn out, but not so – dowdy. In fact, my dear, you look like a Parisienne. The Germans won't recognise you. Lift your chin, Madeleine, and walk through the streets with confidence.'

15

October 1943

Noor loved her new look. It had felt so normal to sit in a hairdressing salon and to try on new clothes, and she couldn't resist peeking at her reflection when she passed a shop window. Perhaps Viennot was right. Perhaps she could blend into the natives of Paris who, despite the war, were always elegant.

But she was wrong about blending in.

A few days later, she was walking quickly through the narrow streets of Le Marais. It was dusk and she was feeling the October chill. Noor was tired, having zigzagged across Paris several times. She had a headache, and the suitcase was heavy as it bumped against her leg. All she could think about was a hot bath and a cold glass of water.

It took a few moments for her to register the ring of metal-tipped boots behind her. There was a rhythm to the way in which they struck the cobbles, matching her speed.

She turned left. The footsteps followed.

She stopped to look in a window. They stopped.

No doubt about it: she was being followed.

How many were there? More than one. Two. Maybe three. Too many to take on, to try to outwit.

'*Halt! Arrêtez!*' a harsh male voice rasped. 'Stop!'

Putting her head down, Noor ran. She swung round a corner and immediately down a dark alleyway. It led into a narrow street, and Noor hurled herself along the pavement and into an open doorway. Pressing herself against a wall, she watched through the cobwebbed window as two Nazi policemen thundered past, their eyes bulging like hunting dogs'.

Noor waited until dark before she crept out. It was close to the curfew hour. She took off her jacket and tied a scarf around her head to disguise herself. There was nothing she could do about the suitcase. There were Germans everywhere: in uniform, in plain clothes, in vans and on foot. Worse than them were the French who collaborated with the Nazis, selling them information.

Had someone been watching her? She'd have to be much more careful.

Keeping to the shadows, she made her way to the Metro, and back to her apartment. She opened the door and fell inside. She felt weak and worn out, and yet the night brought her no sleep.

The next morning she made her way to a small park to meet Viennot and Vaudevire. Her legs were stiff and she approached their bench slowly.

'*Mon Dieu!*' Viennot burst out. 'You look terrible, Madeleine. Black rings around your eyes. Pale, emaciated, shaky.'

She told them what had happened the night before. A look passed between the two men.

'OK,' Vaudevire said. 'The time has come. You will not refuse.'

'Refuse what?'

'You'll go to Normandy. To a farm. You'll be well looked after. Far away from the cat-and-mouse game you're involved in.'

Noor folded her arms. 'I'm not going. You can't make me. I've too much to do.'

Viennot frowned. 'You're behaving like an adolescent. You're exhausted. One slip-up and the Nazis will grab you. And if they capture you, they capture more than just you.'

Vaudevire nodded.

Noor looked down at her feet. They were right.

She was risking more than her own life. And a rest in peaceful countryside might be just what she needed. She sighed, and raised her hands in submission. 'OK,' she said. 'I give in.'

The next day, Vaudevire saw her on to the train at Gare St Lazare. He waited until the doors were shut and the train began to move. Noor smiled. He was making sure she was really going.

She arrived at Le Havre as planned, and was taken by the farmer and his wife to their farmhouse in the middle of the countryside. They kept trying to feed her fresh bread and newly churned butter, home-made cheese, and sweet *galettes*. But Noor had no appetite. Night was darker in the countryside than in Paris, and the silence kept her awake.

Two days later, she took herself back to Paris. She went to meet Viennot at his favourite café.

'Madeleine!' Viennot exclaimed. 'We sent you away. What are you doing here?'

'I couldn't stay on the farm a moment longer. I kept thinking of everything I could be doing here. So.' She rapped the table twice. 'What's my next task?'

Viennot shook his head. 'No, Madeleine. I've heard from my sources that you're the Nazis' prize target.

They're offering a great deal of money for you. You can't work in Paris any longer. It's too dangerous for all of us.' He tapped his cigarette out on his saucer. '*You* are too dangerous for all of us.'

Noor stared at him. 'B-but I'm the only radio operator in Paris – '

'*Non.*' He stubbed out his cigarette. 'You must make arrangements to return to England. As soon as possible.'

16

October 1943

There was no point arguing. Noor could see that she would have to do as he said. Disappointed not to be able to carry on, but also not wanting want to endanger anyone's life, she had mixed feelings.

Lie low until the 14th of October, London said when she radioed. *Then take the Lysander back to England.*

Once again, Noor had had to move – this time into a room in an apartment on the Avenue Foch. Now she was living directly opposite the Gestapo headquarters.

Noor looked out of her window. She'd stayed in the flat for five days, but soon she'd be leaving this view of the majestic building, and its menacing occupants. Many agents had been taken to that building to be interrogated. She shuddered. Turning away, she sorted through her things. Rose petals from the Jourdans' tree fell out of a pocket, still faintly scented. Smiling, she tucked them away in the fold of a dress. She found, too, the envelope with the four special pills Miss Atkins had given her. She rolled them in her hand, remembering the evening when she'd been given them. So much had happened since then. At least she hadn't had to use them. She dropped them back in their envelope and put it in her suitcase to take back. Another agent might need them.

She spent the next two days making her way across Paris, saying goodbye to her friends. It was hardest of all to leave the Jourdans.

'Send our love to your family,' they said. Madame Jourdan had tears in her eyes as she crushed Noor against her.

'I can't wait to see them all myself,' Noor said, and the strength of Madame Jourdan's embrace brought with it the full force of her longing for Amma. Soon she would be back with her. She couldn't wait to hug her, and brush her hair, and read soothing poetry to her.

Noor took a deep breath. 'Thank you for everything,' she said. 'I'll be back to see you when this is all over!' And, turning quickly, she left before they saw she was crying too.

The day before she was due to fly back to England, Noor woke early. There was a bakery on the ground floor of her building, and the warm smells weaving their way upwards made her feel hungry for the first time in weeks. A baguette for breakfast – her last taste of Paris. Perhaps she could even bring one back for Amma. On her way downstairs, she passed a man in a well-cut suit, elegant as only a Frenchman could be. She'd seen him a few times in the street nearby. He tipped his hat to her.

'*Bonjour, Mademoiselle,*' he said with a smile. 'Where are you off to this fine morning?'

'To buy myself my breakfast from the bakery downstairs.'

'Ah.' He sniffed deeply. 'The smell of France. Nothing like it anywhere else in the world. *Bon appétit!*'

He replaced his hat, and trotted up the stairs.

She joined the snaking queue into the bakery. When she finally made it to the counter, there were only a few rolls left. She bought a couple, and left the shop, thinking she'd walk to a café nearby and buy a cup of pretend coffee.

October already, and russet leaves twirled around her from the trees that lined the avenue. She'd be walking in London soon, cosy in a woolly hat and scarf, and watching the ducks in one of the parks with her sister.

Hurried footsteps behind her made her look over her shoulder. Two men in long coats. She was being followed.

Again.

Gathering all her energy, Noor turned the corner, slipped into a dress shop and out through a side door on to another street.

Then she ran.

Dodging people, trees, bicycles, she flew down the streets and round corners, down dark passageways and through shadowed courtyards. Finally, she reached an abandoned building site and threw herself behind some scaffolding. Crouching, struggling for breath, she waited, watching for her followers. It was so annoying that they were pursuing her now. Her time in Paris was over, for heaven's sake, and she was about to leave.

Time passed. She must have lost them. Keeping to the back streets, she made her way back towards her flat. She waited at the end of the street for a few moments. No sign of her pursuers. There'd be no more of this after tomorrow. She leapt up the stairs, took her key out of her pocket, and unlocked her door.

Hands grabbed her. Pushed her down to the floor.

'You?' Noor screamed. 'Traitor! Collaborator!' It was the elegant French man she'd seen earlier on the stairs.

Noor struck at him and punched. He crushed her hands between his fists.

In a fury of biting, scratching and kicking, she hurled herself at him. Again and again, she sank her teeth into his wrists. She spat his blood back at him.

There was a clank of metal. Handcuffs.

'No!' she screamed, flailing her arms, pounding her fists into any part of him she could reach. 'No!'

'Stop!' he said. And he pointed a pistol at her.

Terrified, Noor shuffled backwards.

'Get on the sofa!' he ordered. 'One move, and I'll shoot.'

The gun aimed at her head, he telephoned for help.

Choking with angry sobs and wild fury, Noor screamed at him, and then at the Nazi officers who burst into the flat.

'*Sales Boches!* Filthy Germans!' she swore, hissing and clawing at them as they grabbed her arms and dragged her out of the flat, down the stairs and into the black car idling in the street.

17

13 October 1943

It was a short drive to the Gestapo Headquarters, but a long way from the Paris Noor knew. Four guards shoved her up five flights of stairs and into an office.

'I am Ernst Vogt,' said the German officer standing behind his desk. A creepy smile, oily with triumph, spread across his overfed face.

Noor snarled. Her fists curled and uncurled. If not for the brutes holding her back, she would have thrown herself at him and scratched his beady little eyes out.

'So tell me, *mademoiselle*, what is your name?' he asked. 'Your code name?' He leaned towards her, his greasy lips peeling back to reveal yellow teeth. 'You are Madeleine, aren't you? Aren't you?'

He repeated the questions in French and in English.

Noor glared at him.

'Thought so. Who do you work with?'

'I will not answer your questions!' She spat the words out in French. She did not want him to know she spoke English.

'What are their names? Code names?' He paced in front of her. His breath stank of wine – doubtless French wine.

Noor stayed silent.

'Who arranges the safe houses? Who do you meet? Who gives you instructions?'

Noor only sneered.

He kept firing questions at her, but Noor focussed on a smudge of dirt on the wall behind him. If she did not speak, she would not be lying.

Finally, he stopped pacing. 'All right, *mademoiselle*. Have it your way. For now.' He ordered the guard to take her to a cell.

The guards grabbed her arms. 'I want a bath,' Noor said, elbowing their rough hands off her.

Vogt raised his eyebrows, but gave the guards a nod. They shoved her towards a bathroom. She stepped inside, then turned. The guards had left the door slightly open, and were peering through the crack. She launched herself at the door, pushing it against the foot of one of the guards.

'I won't have anyone watching me,' she screamed. 'Shut the damn door. Now!'

Vogt appeared, and ordered the guard to shut the door.

Immediately, Noor clambered on to the window sill and swung out of the bathroom, balancing on a gutter that circled the building beneath the attic windows. Holding on to the roof tiles, she crept along on silent feet.

She had to get away. She had to catch that flight and go back to England. It was all she could think about.

'Madeleine.' It was Vogt, leaning out of the next window. 'You'll kill yourself,' he said quietly. 'Think of your mother. Here. Take my hand.'

Noor looked down at Avenue Foch, dizzyingly far below. She thought of Amma. Reluctantly, she took his hand, and he pulled her inside, and pushed her into a cell.

The key turned in the lock.

Noor sank on to the hard bed, put her head in her hands and began to sob.

She'd been so close to going home. Why had she walked into their trap? Why had she been such a coward? Why hadn't she let herself fall? Death would have been better than prison – and torture.

Again and again, day after day, Vogt questioned Noor. When she spoke, she told him only what he already knew. And she made it her business to make as much of a fuss as possible. She demanded that the Germans fetch her clothes and soap and makeup and toothpaste from her apartment, and she smoked the cigarettes Vogt gave her. But she refused to tell him what he wanted to know – even when he showed her that he'd worked out her security codes.

Once he shocked her by showing her copies of her letters to Amma.

She'd been betrayed. Which of her fellow agents had it been?

And her precious letters to Amma, whom she missed so deeply, had been read by the Nazis. Noor felt dirtied and used. In the night, these things made her cry, but still she gave nothing away.

Time passed. No doubt the Nazis were sending messages pretending they were from her. Surely London would have realised by now that she'd been captured. How many unsuspecting agents were falling into the German traps?

Noor's cell was dark and stuffy and small. Through the window she could hear the sounds of Paris – so near, so far. She paced the cramped space, angry, frustrated, desperate. She had to get out of there.

One evening, she heard male voices through the wall, the slam of the door, and the grind of a key in the lock: another prisoner. Noor waited until the early hours of the morning. Her neighbour was pacing his cell.

She tapped out a message in Morse Code on the wall.

My name is Madeleine. British agent. Who are you?

He tapped back. *Léon Faye. Also British agent.*

I want to escape. Trying to work out plan.

Count me in.

For the first time in weeks, Noor smiled.

A few days later, she made contact with another prisoner living opposite her: John Starr. He'd heard her crying in the night, and managed to slip a note under her door: *Check under basin in bathroom for more notes*. He was an artist who'd decided to cooperate with the Gestapo, which meant he had access to paper and pencils.

Soon, she, Faye and Starr were leaving notes to each other in the bathroom they shared.

Have escape plan, Starr wrote soon afterwards.

18

November 1943

Small window in ceiling. Could loosen frame with screwdriver, Starr wrote.

Noor's heart plummeted. She'd been staring at her own window for weeks. Its iron bars were tightly screwed in. How on earth did Starr think he could get hold of a screwdriver?

Screwdriver??? she wrote back.

Don't despair. Something will turn up.

Don't despair? Ridiculous. Did he think the Gestapo would simply hand over a tool kit?

A few days later, Starr's note was one word long: *Success!!!!*

He'd tricked the cleaner into giving him a screwdriver so that he could fix her carpet sweeper. He hid it behind the basin, so the three of them could take it in turns to use it.

Noor couldn't reach her window. Her bed was the kind that folded into the wall. Standing on it when it was flat was no use: she just wasn't tall enough. She had to clamber on to the frame when it was folded away, and then lean across to get at the screws.

It was going well. The three bars nearest to her were loose. There was just one to go…

The thud when she hit the floor brought the guards running into her room, pistols cocked.

'What's going on here?'

'Oh… I was… going to… I wanted to hang myself,' Noor said, rubbing her neck.

The guards looked at each other. 'That's just stupid,' one said. 'Don't try that again.'

They left the room without noticing the loosened bars. Immediately, Noor went back to work.

The three kept preparing their escape. Noor shared her face powder with the others so that they could plug the holes left by the loosened bars, and passed on some Metro tickets she'd found in the pockets of her clothes.

It was time. They were all ready. One last screw remained on Noor's window. Starr whistled to cover up the scraping noise as Noor struggled with the final bar. Faye was already through his window. He leant through Noor's and helped her, pulling her up and on to the roof.

Fresh air. Noor almost shouted with joy.

It was cold, and the night sky was dark with shredded cloud. They tiptoed across the rooftop, their shoes tied by their laces and strung round their necks, and blankets slung over their shoulders. Noor moved quickly, ahead of the two men. Her training all those months ago in how to move silently and swiftly had come in useful.

'OK,' Noor whispered. 'We've reached the roof of the next door building. Time for the ropes.'

Quickly, they began to rip the blankets to knot together. 'Hurry!' Noor almost danced with impatience as Faye fumbled with his length of fabric.

The sudden ack-ack-ack of anti-aircraft guns stuttered through the dark. Straight away, long wheeling searchlights probed the sky.

Noor looked up. 'An air raid! Duck!'

The three flung themselves flat on the rooftop. The first thing the guards did when there was an air raid was to check the cells. The alarm would be raised by now.

'Let's make a run for it!' Noor said. 'No choice.'

She stood up and, pulling on her shoes, she led the men back to the edge. She tied an end of the knotted blanket to a drainpipe, and tested it briefly. Then, gripping it, she swung into the window of the building below. Her feet smashed through the glass and she landed amongst the shards. Faye and Starr followed.

Had anyone heard them? No time to find out. They ran out of the room, through the door and down the main staircase. Starr opened the front door a crack. He peered out, then shut the door immediately, his eyes wide.

'Gestapo outside. We're trapped.'

'Let's run. See how far we get,' Faye said.

'Yes,' Noor said. 'Let's go.'

She opened the door, and they hurtled out into the street. Faye was ahead. He'd just reached the corner when the Germans opened fire. Starr grabbed Noor and dragged her back into the house. Her heart pounding, she made for the stairs. A woman, her face moon-white, stared down at them from a floor above.

Before Noor could say a word, the front door exploded and jackboots thumped up the stairs. Hands grabbed Noor by the hair, yanking her backwards. She was thrown to the floor, kicked in the ribs, punched in the back and stomach. She tried to curl into a bundle.

She was lifted and hauled out of the house, and back next door to the Gestapo headquarters, and another cell.

19

November 1943 to September 1944

The door to her cell was flung open. It was agony to sit up, but Noor didn't want to look weak.

A big man, heavy-footed, his uniform crisp and buttons shiny, strode in.

'I am Kieffer, head of the Paris Gestapo,' he said in thickly-accented French. He was holding a piece of paper. 'So, *mademoiselle*. I heard you had a little outing. Did you enjoy it?'

Noor glared at him.

'This is a document.' He fluttered the paper at her. 'A promise that you will not try to escape again. If you sign this, you may stay here in Avenue Foch.'

Noor didn't bother looking at his paper. 'I will not sign it.'

It hurt to breathe, but nevertheless she inhaled deeply. She wanted her voice to be strong.

'I will always keep trying to escape, because that is my duty. If I signed your – your document, it would be a lie. I do not lie.'

Kieffer whacked the side of his leg with the paper. His eyes were chips of granite. 'I see. Too bad.' He called an officer to the cell. '*Mademoiselle* is going to Pforzheim Prison. See to it at once. She is a highly dangerous prisoner. *Nacht und Nebel – Rückkehr Unerwünscht.*'

Noor knew what that meant: Night and fog – return not required. She was going to 'disappear'. None of her friends or family would know where she was. Noor's vision began to blot out and everything became fuzzy.

Abba, please help me, she thought. *I need your strength.* One of his songs wound its way into her mind, an Indian raga he'd taught her, and it was as if he were there with her.

Calm now, she squared her shoulders, and raised her chin in defiance. She would not give Kieffer the satisfaction of seeing how upset she was.

Armed guards seized her and threw her into an army truck. She was driven through the night across France and into Germany to her new prison.

Pforzheim was a huge institution, a chunk of architecture. She was shoved into a cell set apart from others by fences and locked gates, and bolted in.

Noor stood, numb, looking at her new home. The iron bed had a worn mattress, no thicker than an old blanket. A rusting bucket stood in the corner – her loo. The room was dank and dark, weak light coming from a tiny window high above, and it stank of urine, and air that had been breathed too often.

She'd only been there a few minutes when the door was unlocked. There was clanking as two guards brought in some lengths of chain.

'Get up!' one ordered, kicking her feet.

'Say please,' Noor retorted in German.

'Don't speak!'

They handcuffed her, chained her ankles together and her hands to her feet. The heavy iron was cold and pressed against Noor's bruises and cuts. The door was banged close, and with the slam of the bolts, any seedlings of hope Noor might have had were viciously stamped out.

Tears smarted Noor's eyes. 'Stop it,' she told herself. She wiped them off on her shoulder, the chains clanging as she did so.

Her days were endless, broken only by the visits of the male warden who brought her bowls of thin gruel to eat, and the female warden with hands like potato graters who fed her and cleaned her. The lights went off in the early evening, and long nights would then follow long days.

Noor grew steadily weaker. She forced herself to walk backwards and forwards across her cell, the weight of the chains becoming increasingly difficult to bear. It was only the thought of her family, and her memories of Abba's wise teaching, that kept her mind straight.

Noor was waiting one afternoon for someone to collect her used metal bowl when she noticed scratching on the base. When she held it up to the light, she made out some writing.

There are three girls here, it said.

Noor laughed out loud. She'd heard activity in the corridor outside her cell.

How could she reply? She needed something sharp. She darted a glance around the room. Nothing. Could she somehow use her handcuffs? No, but her finger nails were long and brittle. They might do.

She tried.

Yes. Her writing looked like runes, but it worked. *You are not alone, you have a friend in Cell 1,* she replied.

They sent messages to each other. Sometimes it took days to receive them when the bowls were used by other prisoners. Noor tried to keep her spirits up by making up stories in her head, and remembering those that Abba had told. But in the long, cold nights, misery would often overcome her, and she would weep into the prickly blanket.

The daylight hours began to shorten again. Noor reckoned she must have been there almost a year. Late one afternoon, the female warden scuttled into her cell and removed her clothes. She gave her a rough, sackcloth garment to wear instead.

'Why – what is happening?' Noor asked, breaking the rule of silence.

'You are going,' the warden said.

'Where?'

The warden shrugged her hefty shoulders, bundled up Noor's clothes and left.

I am leaving, Noor wrote, without hope, on her bowl. She knew that her next destination was unlikely to be pleasant.

That evening, Noor was unchained and pushed down the corridors and out of the prison. They stepped outside, and Noor stopped to breathe the autumnal air. She felt weightless without her shackles, as though she might be carried off by a breeze.

'*Schnell*! Quick!' the guard shouted, rapping her on her shoulder blade.

'One moment,' Noor said fiercely. She looked up at the sky. So much light all at once dazzled her eyes. But there was something she wanted to see before she would allow herself to be shoved into the waiting car.

Seconds later, a bird flew across the evening sky as though it had been summoned. Noor looked at it until she couldn't see it any longer, sending with its free wings a message of love to Amma, and to her sister and brothers.

Then she nodded, throwing off the guard's hand on the back of her neck. 'I am going,' she said, getting into the car.

20

12 September 1944

She was driven twenty miles to the office of the head of the Karlsruhe Gestapo.

Three other women were already there, all of them thin and pale. One had a terrible cough that brought a snarl of irritation to the face of the Gestapo officer. The sick woman looked over at Noor. Her eyebrows shot up, and she gave her a wary smile.

Noor stared. It wasn't... It couldn't be, could it?

It was. It was Yolande Beekman. They'd met during their training back in England a hundred years before. Noor put her fingers to her lips and blew her a disguised kiss.

The Gestapo officer's jagged voice sawed through Noor's mixed feelings of joy and fear.

'You will all four leave now. For Dachau. Two officers will accompany you,' he said in French.

Dachau? Were they being taken to another prison? Noor glanced at Yolande, but she didn't seem to know where or what it was.

Forbidden to speak to each other, they were driven to the station, and made to board a train.

Once they were on the way to Munich, their guards let them speak. Noor threw her arms around Yolande. The two of them clung to each other. And then the barrage began: not having spoken to anyone for close to a year, Noor poured out questions. How was the war progressing? Who was winning? Where had the others been? Who had they worked with? How had they been captured?

They exchanged stories, gasping at each other's narrow escapes. Noor told them how she'd been stopped by two Gestapo officers on the Metro, and how she'd pretended her radio set was a cinematographic apparatus.

'They even looked inside the suitcase,' she said. 'Neither knew what it was, but they didn't want to admit it.' She acted out their eyebrow-raising and pretend-knowledgeable grunting, and all four women roared with laughter.

Through the window, the scenery changed. It was like watching a beautiful film.

'Where are we going?' they asked the guards.

'To a camp,' they said. 'Where there is farming.'

They were given lunch, and cigarettes, and all four women felt light-hearted, as though they were on holiday. It was dark when their train finally slowed, and stopped.

'Out!' the guards ordered. The holiday was over.

The women stepped out into an eerily silent place of lined-up sheds, watchtowers, barbed wire fences. And a stink of rot and sewage so thick Noor felt she was being smothered.

She bent over and vomited.

Gagging too, Yolande put her arm around her.

'Stop that! Walk!' shouted the guard.

They stumbled through a gate. The metalwork sign above it read *Arbeit Macht Frei*. Work makes one free, Noor translated. What work?

Other guards appeared, with German shepherd dogs. With the butts of their rifles, they separated the women, shoving them in different directions.

'Bye!' Noor called out to the others. Their replies were stifled. She was herded into a cell. The door slammed, and was bolted three times. When Noor turned round, there was a man waiting for her.

Then the longest night of her life began.

21

13 September 1944

The icy fingers of dawn touched the bars of the prison cell, before feeling their way to Noor's body slumped across the cement floor.

'Kneel!' the Nazi officer ordered in his coarse French accent, shoving her feet with his boot.

Slowly, her breath rasping in her throat, she pushed against the floor until she'd raised her upper body. Using every last atom of her strength, she lifted her head until she looked the officer in the eye.

He put the pistol to her temple. The metal was so beautifully cold.

He cocked the trigger.

A small smile flickered at her lips. '*Liberté*,' she said, before he fired one single shot.

Epilogue

Noor Inayat Khan sacrificed her life to serve the country which had sheltered her family. She remained true to her beliefs even when viciously tortured by the Nazis, never lying and never informing on others. Radio operators were not expected to survive more than a few weeks, yet she not only carried on for four months, but did the work of about six operators at a time when the Germans were actively pursuing her.

We do not know who betrayed Noor. Some believe that it may have been Renée Garry, Henri Garry's sister, who was jealous of Noor and of her friendship with Antelme, but Renée was found not guilty in a trial held after the war. Noor may have been betrayed by another agent, either a double agent working both for the SOE and the Nazis, or even a fellow agent who revealed her identity under torture.

Of the agents mentioned in this account, only Marguerite Garry, Viennot, Gieules, Germaine Aigrain, Professor Balachowsky and John Starr survived the war. The rest were all killed by the Nazis, most of them, like Noor, in concentration camps.

Himmler, Hitler's right-hand man, ordered that all secret agents should be executed, but only after they had been tortured into revealing every scrap of information that would enable the Germans to arrest other agents.

After Noor's death, in recognition of her courage, her loyalty and her determination, the British awarded her the George Cross. The French, too, conferred on her the highest civilian award: the Croix de Guerre with Gold Star. In Gordon Square, London, close to the house where she lived in 1914, a statue of Noor has been erected in memory of her life and her contribution to Britain.

Also available...

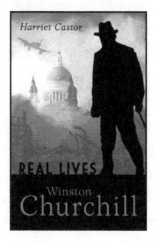

From soldier to MP to international war correspondent, Winston Churchill always has to be at the centre of the action. But following a turbulent career in politics, Churchill is faced with the worst war the world has ever seen. And this time, *he's* in charge.

Real Lives are narrative accounts of the life and times of some of the world's most iconic figures.

ISBN: 978-1-4081-3117-6
RRP: £5.99

Also available...

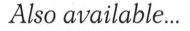

One of the most influential thinkers of the 20th century, Alan Turing is considered to be the father of computer science and artificial intelligence. His work cracking the 'unbreakable' Enigma code in World War II saved millions of lives, yet he tragically lost his own in the face of prejudice.

Real Lives are narrative accounts of the life and times of some of the world's most iconic figures.

ISBN: 978-1-4729-0010-4

RRP: £5.99